Victor's Pink Pyjamas

Editor: Ellen Turnbull
Cover and Interior: Cyrus Gandevia
Illustrations: William Kimber
Proofreader: Dianne Greenslade

CopperHouse is an imprint of Wood Lake Publishing, Inc.
Wood Lake Publishing acknowledges the financial
support of the Government of Canada, through the Book
Publishing Industry Development Program (BPIDP) for its publishing activities.
Wood Lake Publishing also acknowledges the financial support of the Province of
British Columbia through the Book Publishing Tax Credit.

At Wood Lake Publishing, we practise what we publish, being guided by a concern
for fairness, justice, and equal opportunity in all of our relationships with employees
and customers. Wood Lake Publishing is committed to caring for the environment
and all creation. Wood Lake Publishing recycles, reuses, and encourages readers
to do the same. Resources are printed on 100% post-consumer recycled paper and
more environmentally friendly groundwood papers (newsprint) whenever possible.
A percentage of all profit is donated to charitable organizations.

Library and Archives Canada Cataloguing in Publication

Alary, Laura, 1970-, author
    Victor's pink pyjamas / Laura Alary ; illustrated by
William Kimber.

ISBN 978-1-77064-571-4 (pbk.)

    I. Kimber, William, 1945-, illustrator II. Title.

PS8601.L364V52 2013   jC813'.6   C2013-902579-0

Published by CopperHouse
An imprint of Wood Lake Publishing Inc.
9590 Jim Bailey Road, Kelowna, BC, Canada, V4V 1R2
www.woodlakebooks.com
250.766.2778

Printing 10 9 8 7 6 5 4 3 2 1
Printed in Canada
by Houghton Boston

Laura Alary

Illustrated By
William Kimber

Victor's Pink Pyjamas

CopperHouse

Victor's pyjamas were not always pink. When Grandma made them they were creamy white, like French vanilla ice cream. But they got washed with his sister's red socks and came out pink.

"Oh Victor," cried his mother, "I'm so sorry!"

"Never mind," soothed Grandma, "I'll make you another pair."

But Victor *loved* his pink pyjamas. When he put them on he felt happy and silly, and joy rose in him like bubbles in a fizzy drink.

Victor's father was not pleased about the pyjamas.

"He can't wear those!" he declared to Victor's mother.
"Pink is for girls!"

"Why just for girls?" asked Victor.

"I don't know why, it just is."

"Walruses are pink," said Victor, "and they're not just for girls."

"Walruses are not pink, they're grey," retorted his father.

"Only in the water," explained Victor. "When they lie on rocks in the sun they turn pink. That's because they're warm and happy, like me in my pyjamas."

"Did you hear that?" Victor's grandma said to his father. "The pink pyjamas make him happy. For goodness sake, let the boy be."

Victor's father sighed, but agreed that Victor could wear his pink pyjamas at home when it was just family around.

It was winter and Victor's sister's birthday was coming up. She planned to go skating with her friends, then come home for hot chocolate and pizza and cake. Victor wanted to stay up and have hot chocolate too.

"All right, Victor," said his sister. "But don't wear your pink pyjamas or my friends will make fun of you."

On the night of the party, Victor wore his pink pyjamas anyway.

"Why is your brother wearing pink pyjamas?" she giggled. "Pink is for girls!"

"Why just for girls?" asked Victor.

"I don't know why," she said, "it just is."

Victor looked down at his plate of hot buttered toast.

"Crabapple jelly is pink," he said, "and it's not just for girls."

The girl stared at him.

"Lots of things are pink and not just for girls," Victor explained. "Like Grandma's crabapple jelly. Or my dog's tongue when he kisses me. Or the sky in winter just before dark. Or my cheeks when I come in from sledding."

"Whatever," sniffed the girl. But she said nothing else about Victor's pink pyjamas.

In the spring, Victor was invited to his very first sleepover.

"He'll need new pyjamas," declared his father. "There's no way he can wear those pink things. The other boys will laugh at him."

Victor wore his pink pyjamas anyway and the other boys
did laugh at him.

"Why are you wearing pink pyjamas?" they chortled.
"Pink is for girls!"

"Why just for girls?" asked Victor.

"We don't know why, it just is."

"Worms are pink," argued Victor. "So are the naked mole rats at the zoo. And baby birds in the nest. Pencil erasers are pink. Strawberry ice cream is pink too. Those things aren't just for girls."

Nobody teased Victor the rest of the night.

At the end of the school year, Victor's class had a party. Everyone was supposed to wear pyjamas and bring a favourite stuffed animal to school.

The night before the party, Victor set out his pink pyjamas and his stuffed pig.

"Victor," warned his father, glancing in the room, "there is no way you are wearing those pink pyjamas to school. I absolutely forbid it."

Victor wore the pink pyjamas to school anyway. He caused quite a stir among the boys and girls in his class.

"Why are you wearing pink pyjamas, Victor?" they hooted. "Pink is for girls!"

"Why just for girls?" asked Victor.

"We don't know why, it just is."

"Well, think about it," said Victor. "Cherry Popsicles are pink. Starfish are pink. So are the insides of shells. Wild roses, and fireworks, and mosquito bites, and calamine lotion – all pink! Those things are not just for girls. They're for everyone!"

No one said another word about the pink pyjamas.

That summer, Victor wore his pink pyjamas at the cottage and when he slept out in the tent in the backyard. He loved them as much as ever. But as fall drew near, even Victor had to admit that the pink pyjamas were too small.

"Good," declared his father. "Let's turn those old things into rags and get you a proper pair."

But Victor was not ready to give up his pyjamas, tight and threadbare though they were.

Then, the night before school began, Grandma handed Victor a package.

"Victor," she said, "you have grown so much that I thought I should make you a new pair of pyjamas."

"Thank goodness," said Victor's father. "It's about time we put an end to this foolishness."

"Oh, Grandma!" cried Victor as he tore open the package.
"I love them!"

"Just for you, my dear boy," she said. "Because flamingos are pink, and bubblegum, and hot dogs – and they're not just for girls, are they?"